Lalaloopsy™
Sew Magical! Sew Cute!

Halloween Surprise

D0580527

by Lauren Cecil

SCHOLASTIC INC.

New York   Toronto   London   Auckland   Sydney   Mexico City   New Delhi   Hong Kong

ISBN 978-0-545-43388-4

12 11 10 9 8 7 6 5 4 3 2 1

12 13 14 15 16 17/0

Designed by Angela Jun
Printed in the U.S.A.
First printing, July 2012

40

It was almost Halloween. Red and yellow leaves fell from the trees. The air was cool and crisp.

Misty Mysterious, Dot Starlight, Jewel Sparkles, Bea Spells-a-Lot, and Pillow Featherbed were in a pumpkin patch. They were searching for the perfect pumpkin to carve.

Misty found a great, big pumpkin. Then she noticed something strange. There was a note pinned to the pumpkin. "Hey, guys!" she called to her friends. "Check this out!"

Everyone ran over to take a look. "What is it?" Pillow asked. "I think it's a riddle," Misty said. The she read the note aloud. "'A special Halloween scavenger hunt, you're about to begin. What's brown and fluffy, and hard to find a needle in?'"

Everyone thought very hard.
"A haystack is brown, fluffy, and hard to find a needle in!" exclaimed Bea. "Let's go!"

They ran off to search for their next clue.

The girls arrived at the haystacks, and Jewel found another clue. "'I make birds fly away and caw,'" she read. "'Can you find me? I'm made of straw.'"

"I know!" Dot cried. "Scarecrows are made of straw, and they scare away birds."

"All right," Bea said. "Let's go!"

As the girls dashed over to the scarecrows, Pillow lagged behind.

"What's wrong?" Dot asked.

"The sun's going down, and I feel kind of scared," Pillow admitted. "You can use my flashlight," Dot said. "It will make you feel less afraid."

With the help of the flashlight, Pillow found the next clue. "'I'm a crunchy Halloween treat,'" she read. "'I'm red and shiny, and good to eat!'"

"I know!" Misty cried. "It's an apple. Let's go to the apple orchard!" Everyone ran to the apple orchard, with Pillow leading the way.

The apple orchard was very dark and very spooky. Strange sounds filled the air.

Then suddenly, everything went dark.
"Oh, no!" Pillow shouted. "The battery went out!"
"Don't worry," Dot said. "I have an extra one somewhere."

"There!" Dot said after she changed the battery. "That's much better!"

Pillow turned on the flashlight. "Look!" she said. "It's a trail made of candy."

"And it leads to another clue!" Dot said pointing to a tree. "'A spooky Halloween surprise awaits,'" Bea read. "'Follow the trail, and don't be late!'"

"**A**re you sure this is a good idea?" Jewel asked.
"We've already come this far," Dot added.
"All right," Pillow agreed. "If we stick together everything will be okay."

The girls followed the candy trail until it ended at a big barn door. "What should we do now?" Misty asked.

"Let's see if anyone's inside," Dot suggested. She cracked open the door. "Hello?"

Suddenly, a skeleton appeared out of the darkness and shouted, "BOO!"

"*Ahhhh!*" shrieked Pillow, Misty, Jewel, Bea, and Dot.

Then the lights flashed on.
The skeleton was Patch Treasurechest dressed in costume!

"We wanted to make a spooky Halloween party for all our friends," said Patch.

"We hope we didn't scare you too much!" Berry Jars 'n' Jam added.

"You sure tricked us," said Jewel.

"**A**nd now I'm ready for some treats," said Pillow.
"Let's party!" said Dot.

At the party, there were yummy treats to eat and fun Halloween games to play.

There were even silly costumes for everyone to try on.

"**S**orry we scared you," Berry said.

"We only wanted to have a little fun," added Patch.

"We were pretty frightened," Pillow admitted. "But being with our friends made us feel a lot better."

"This is one Halloween we'll never forget!" Jewel added.